NORMAN BRIDWELL

Clifford®
TO THE RESCUE

SCHOLASTIC INC.

New York   Toronto   London   Auckland   Sydney
Mexico City   New Delhi   Hong Kong

To
Daniel Jacob Morris
—N.B.

ISBN 0-439-14038-2

10 9 8 7 6 5 4 3 2   00 01 02 03 04 05

Printed in the U.S.A.   24
First printing, March 2000

I'm Emily Elizabeth and this is my dog, Clifford.

Clifford likes to eat.

And he likes to play.

But most of all,
Clifford likes to help.

A kitten was in danger,

Clifford was right there.

And when Clifford's friends were trapped behind a fence . . .

Clifford came to the rescue.

Clifford's brother Nero is also very helpful.

Nero is a rescue dog at a fire station.

Clifford and I visited him.

While we were there, the alarm rang.
We followed the fire truck. Nero rushed
into the building.

Clifford helped him.

One day, Clifford and I saw a
sign that said the circus was in town.
A smaller sign said the circus needed help.

So Clifford slipped into an elephant suit
and gave them a hand. I mean, a tail.

Last year, our town celebrated its
birthday with a big parade.

Suddenly, a man ran up and stopped the parade.

There was trouble ahead at the bridge.

Clifford and I rushed off as fast as we could go.

Oh, no! The bridge had collapsed.
Clifford did some quick thinking.
Can you guess what happened then?

The big parade went on as planned,
but Clifford wasn't in it. . . .

He was under it!

One day, I was walking my big red dog
when a car came speeding past us.

And right behind it came a police car.
The police were chasing robbers.

Clifford took a short cut . . .

and caught the robbers.

The police were happy.

I'm so proud of my big red dog.

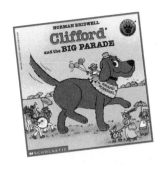

Look for the pictures from
Clifford to the Rescue
in these other funny books!

Clifford and the Big Parade

Clifford at the Circus

Clifford Gets a Job

Clifford's Birthday Party

Clifford's Family

Clifford's Good Deeds

Clifford's Kitten

Clifford's Pals

Clifford's Riddles

Happy reading!

Norman Bridwell's career got off to a big start with the publication of CLIFFORD THE BIG RED DOG. Thirty-seven years and many books later, Mr. Bridwell continues to enchant the picture-book crowd.

What makes Clifford so irresistible? Mr. Bridwell has his own theory: "I think Clifford's success is based on his not being perfect. Clifford always tries to do the right thing, but he does make mistakes."

Norman Bridwell, who was born and raised in Indiana, lives in Martha's Vineyard, Massachusetts.